For my two girls, Korey and Penelope

For information address Disney • Hyperion, 125 West End Avenue, New York, New York 10023.
First Edition, May 2015 • 10 9 8 7 6 • FAC-029191-16221 • Printed in Malaysia

Library of Congress Cataloging-in-Publication Data • Wu, Mike, author, illustrator. • Ellie / Mike Wu.—First edition.   pages   cm
Summary: When zookeeper Walt announces that the zoo will have to close, all of the animals pitch in to try to save their home but it is Ellie the elephant who reveals a talent that just may keep the zoo open for good. • ISBN 978-1-4847-1239-9—ISBN 1-4847-1239-0 [1. Elephants—Fiction. 2. Zoos—Fiction. 3. Artists—Fiction. 4. Zoo animals—Fiction.]
I. Title. • PZ7.W96225Ell 2015 • [E]—dc23 • 2014015778

Reinforced binding • Visit www.DisneyBooks.com

Ellie

by Mike Wu

 · HYPERION   Los Angeles   New York

On a bright winter day, when Ellie was just finishing her lunch, the zookeeper came by with an announcement.

"Gather 'round!" Walt called. "I have some news."

"It is a sad day," he said.
"The zoo is closing."

The animals were heartbroken.

"There must be something we can do," Ellie
whispered to her friends. "The zoo is our home."

"Perhaps we can spruce it up a bit," Gerard suggested.
Gerard always had good ideas.

"I'll prune the trees," Lucy said, nibbling a leaf.

"If only my trunk were longer!" said Ellie.

"I'll move this rock," Gerard huffed, clearing it off the path.

"If only my muscles were bigger!" said Ellie.

"We've already cleaned here,"
said the monkeys.

"What can I do to help?"
Ellie wondered.

It seemed like everyone had a talent.

Everyone
but Ellie.

Ellie thought she'd ask Walt to give
her a job, but he was busy too.

When the monkeys called him away, Ellie picked up the strange object he'd been holding. It had smooth wood on one side and prickly hairs on the other.

Ellie gave it a try!

When Walt returned and saw her creation, he sprinted back down the path without a word.

Had she ruined the wall?

Soon she heard a wagon with a squeaky wheel turn the corner.

Maybe Walt *did* like her painting!

Ellie added color here . . .

and a rainbow there.

There were so many walls to color,
and so many colors to try!

Ellie painted all of her friends.

She painted the tallest ones . . .

the smartest . . .

and the quietest ones.

Word spread of Ellie's talents.

Squeak!

ROAR!

chirp

People came from all over the city to have their portraits painted.

Some came with balloons.

Others came with awards.

Ellie even painted Mr. Mayor with a smile.

Soon, people from around the world came to
see Ellie, the remarkable painting elephant.

Lucy hosted the crowds as they arrived at the zoo.

Ellie's Gallery

Gerard led tours
through Ellie's art gallery.

And on a bright spring day, with crowds cheering him on,
Walt declared: "We are open for good!"

Thanks to *Ellie!*